playhouse
Disney
Encyclopedia

365 FACTS FOR LEARNING FUN!

Disney PRESS
New York

Parent's Note

This comprehensive encyclopedia is specially designed for the active preschool learner, eager to explore the Earth they live on, the animals they share the planet with, and the elements of nature that surround them.

★ The Mickey Mouse Clubhouse pals present fascinating information about all the many wonders of the Earth.

★ Handy Manny and the tools share their sense of excitement and fun as they explore the animal world.

★ Winnie the Pooh and friends introduce amazing facts about some pretty Tiggerific things found in nature.

★ The Little Einsteins invite children to enrich and reinforce their newfound knowledge with fun and exciting activity pages.

★ Set your child off on a learning adventure by introducing a fact a day. Each entry in the encyclopedia is numbered, so your child can learn a new fact each day of the year.

★ Throughout this book, children will find their favorite Disney characters on hand to guide them through the various sections. Each set of Disney characters brings a unique voice to the world of amazing discovery that's about to unfold.

What's Inside?

▲ Mother cheetah lying with her cubs

Mammals

A mammal is a type of animal. There are more than four thousand different mammal species that live on earth. You are a mammal, too!

How Are Mammals Born?

Mammals grow inside their mothers until they are born. Most do not hatch from eggs, like birds or reptiles do.

What Are Mammals?

Mammals are animals with hair or fur. Mammals are warm-blooded, which means their bodies always stay the same temperature, no matter what their surroundings.

ack bear

Mammal—that's a nice way to say "lady," isn't it?

No, Pat, you're thinking of the word *ma'am*!

▼ *Piglets feeding from their mother*

Baby-Mammal Diet

Baby mammals drink milk from their mothers.

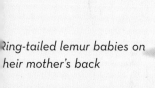

Ring-tailed lemur babies on their mother's back

5

Dog

Fact 1 The dog is often called "man's best friend." That's because dogs are easy to train and make loyal companions.

▼ *Beagle*

Fact 2

Most dogs make great family pets. But did you know that many dogs—such as police or firehouse dogs—live and work side by side with humans?

◄ *Search-and-rescue bloodhound*

Fact 3

Baby dogs are called puppies. Did you know that puppies cannot see or hear for the first two weeks of life? All puppies are born with blue eyes, but their eyes turn a permanent color when they're about one month old.

West Highland white terrier puppies ►

◄ *Jack Russell terrier*

Fact 4

Dogs can hear very high and very low noises that humans cannot. In fact, they can detect sounds that are four times farther away than humans are able to hear!

Rabbit

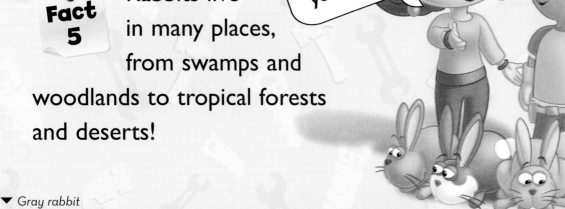

Fact 5

Rabbits live in many places, from swamps and woodlands to tropical forests and deserts!

▼ Gray rabbit

Fact 6

Baby rabbits are called kits. Kits do not have fur when they are born, so they like to snuggle to stay warm and cozy in their dens.

◀ *Kits in their den*

Scrub hare ▶

Fact 7

A rabbit's long ears can turn in any direction to help it hear even the faintest sounds. Rabbits will thump their hind legs to let other rabbits know when they sense danger.

Fact 8

Rabbits usually live in groups in underground burrows. They eat grass, bark, leaves, and berries.

◀ *Snowshoe hare*

Horse

Fact 9

Horses are large, strong mammals with hooves and long manes and tails. Some people use horses for riding, while others, such as farmers, use them to carry heavy loads and pull wagons or plows.

Galloping horses ▼

Fact 10

Baby horses are called foals. Male foals are called colts, and female foals are called fillies. Foals have very long legs relative to their bodies, so they are a bit wobbly and uncoordinated when walking. When they turn one year old, horses are called yearlings.

◀ *Mother and her foal*

Fact 11

Horses are born with no teeth. Between six and nine months of age, foals have all of their baby teeth. Then, just like humans, horses lose their baby teeth at five or six years old when their adult teeth begin to grow in.

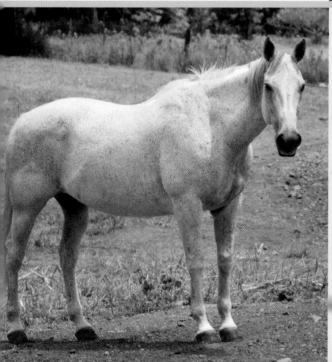

Fact 12

Horses can lock their leg muscles into a stable standing position, so they can sleep standing up without falling over.

Elephant

Fact 13
There are two kinds of elephants: African elephants with very big ears and Asian elephants with smaller ears.

Mommy elephants can be pregnant for two whole years!

African elephant with her calf ▼

12

Fact 14 An elephant uses its trunk for breathing, smelling, and picking up favorite foods—such as hay, grasses, and plant roots—and putting them in their mouths. To clean off, elephants suck water into their trunks and then hose themselves down.

▲ Elephant drinking from a water hole in South Africa

Fact 15 Baby elephants, which are called calves, may use their trunks to hold on to their mothers' tails. Some calves put their trunks in their mouths to soothe themselves, like the way human babies suck their thumbs or pacifiers.

African elephant calf ▶

Fact 16

An elephant's wrinkly skin is very sensitive. Elephants usually roll around in mud and throw dirt on their backs to keep their skin cool and to protect it from sunburn and insect bites.

◀ Indian elephants playing in the mud

13

Swingers

▲ Chimpanzee

Fact 17 Chimpanzees are our closest relatives in the animal world. They show their feelings very much the way humans do. They hug, kiss, smile, and even hold on to each other when sad or scared. They also tickle each other when playing.

Fact 18 Unlike most animals, chimpanzees are able to make and use tools. They use rocks to crack open nuts, and use sticks to smash fruit and dig for ants. Chimpanzees teach their young how to use tools for gathering food.

An animal that can use a tool? Cool!

Fact 19

Chimpanzees have very long arms, which they use to swing from limbs and vines in the dense forests where they live.

◀ Chimpanzee in a tree

Hoppers

Fact 20

Kangaroos are marsupials, which are mammals that carry their babies in pouches outside their stomachs.

◀ *Young red kangaroo*

Fact 21

Baby kangaroos are called joeys. Joeys are about the size of a human thumb when they are born. A joey will nurse and grow in its mother's pouch for almost one year.

Joey in its mother's pouch ▶

Fact 22

Other than low grunts or clucks, kangaroos don't make many noises—but they will thump their back feet to warn another kangaroo of danger. Kangaroos also use their tails for balance when standing, hopping, or kicking.

◀ *Kangaroos in the Blue Mountains, New South Wales, Australia*

Giraffe

Fact 23

Giraffes are the tallest animals in the world, so they are able to reach food where other animals cannot. They use their long necks to reach leaves in the highest branches of trees.

Like human fingerprints, no two giraffes have the same pattern of spots!

▼ Group of giraffes

Fact 24

When baby giraffes are born, they are already taller than many grown-up humans!

◀ A baby giralle is called a calf.

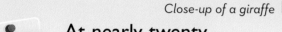

Close-up of a giraffe ▶

Fact 25

At nearly twenty inches in length, a giraffe's long, black tongue wraps around tree branches and pulls off the leaves.

Fact 26

Since it's very hard for them to bend over and lay down on the ground, giraffes can sleep standing up. A giraffe lays down to sleep for less than two hours a day.

◀ A sleepy giraffe

Panda

Pandas are bears with black-and-white fur coats. Most of a panda's body is white, but its arms, legs, ears, and eye patches are usually black. Pandas can only be found living in the wild in one place: China.

Pandas are just like me—they have sharp claws and are very handsome!

A panda eating ▼

18

Fact 28

In China, pandas can be found living in rainy bamboo forests high in the mountains. Unlike other bears (which primarily eat meat), the panda is a plant eater that lives on a diet of bamboo shoots and leaves.

◀ *Panda gets a drink*

Fact 29

Panda cubs are born with all-white fur. Their black spots start to develop when they're one month old. Mother pandas like to wrestle and play with their young cubs.

Mother panda with her cub ▶

Fact 30

Giant pandas have enlarged wrist bones on their front paws that act like opposable thumbs. These "thumbs" help them hold and eat bamboo —pandas' favorite food.

◀ *Panda munching on bamboo*

Lion

Fact 31 Lions are members of the cat family. They live on the savanna together in groups of fifteen to forty lions. These groups are called prides.

I'd be *lion* if I told you I wasn't scared!

Two lion cubs under a bush ▼

Fact 32

Lions are the only cats with manes. Female lions, called lionesses, do not have manes; only the males do. Lions are also the only cats with tufts of hair at the ends of their tails. Is this lion male or female?

◀ *African lion*

Fact 33

In addition to taking turns babysitting and nursing each other's cubs, lionesses usually hunt together as a team for the whole pride.

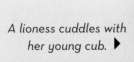

A lioness cuddles with her young cub. ▶

Fact 34

Lions can roar louder than other big cats, such as the leopard, tiger, or jaguar. A lion's roar can be heard up to five miles away! Most lions don't start roaring until they are about two years old.

◀ *A lion roaring*

Polar Bear

Fact 35

Polar bears are the largest bears in the world. They can weigh as much as 1100 pounds or more and stand ten feet tall.

Here's a fun fact: most polar bears are left-handed!

A polar bear scratching his back by rolling in the snow ▼

Fact 36

Polar bears live in Arctic areas with extremely cold weather, such as Alaska, Canada, Russia, Greenland, and Norway.

◀ *Polar bear in sea between ice floes*

 Fact 37 Even though their fur is white, polar bears actually have black skin! Their dark skin helps to absorb the sun's rays and keep them warm. Polar bears also have black noses and lips, and purple tongues.

Polar bear sticking out his tongue ▶

Fact 38

Along with their thick fur, polar bears also have a three-inch layer of blubber under their skin to help keep them warm while swimming in cold water and walking on ice.

◀ *Polar bear mother with her two cubs*

23

Flying Eagle Owl ▶

▼ Sparrows in a nest

Birds

Birds can caw, coo, sing, or chirp. Some birds can even repeat words they hear people say.

How Are Birds Born?

Every bird hatches from an egg.

Hummingbirds lay *huevos* that are about the size of jelly beans!

◀ *Toucan*

What Are Birds?

All birds have wings and feathers, but not all birds can fly. Some just swim, walk, or run.

Pájaro means "bird" in Spanish.

Next to a Phillips-head screwdriver, there's nothing quite as graceful as a *pájaro*!

Ooh, let's learn all about birds!

A paha-row? That doesn't sound like any animal I've ever heard of!

Peacock fanning feathers ▼

How Do Birds Eat?

Birds don't have teeth. They use their sharp beaks to "chew" their food.

Owl

Fact 39

Owls are birds that sleep during the day and hunt for food at night. Their very large eyes allow them to take in more light and see better in the dark. Owls can see up to 100 times better than people!

This guy is a real hoot!

▼ Great horned owl

Fact 40

Baby owls are called owlets. When owlets hatch, their eyes are closed and they are covered with fluffy baby feathers called down.

◀ *Great horned owlets*

Fact 41

Owls have excellent hearing. The owl's ears are hidden under its feathers. If they hear a noise coming from behind them, owls can turn their heads almost all the way around and even upside down to look back.

Tawny owl ▶

Fact 42

Although an owl's feathers make it look very big and plump, owls are actually very lightweight birds. An owl's feathers are so soft that it can fly through the air without making any noise at all.

Flying owl ▶

Little Birds

◀ *Anna's hummingbird*

Fact 43 Hummingbirds are the smallest birds in the world. The tiniest hummingbird, called the bee hummingbird, is only two-and-a-half inches long!

Fact 44 The hummingbird can rotate its wings in a circle, making it the only bird able to move up, down, forward, backward, and sideways. They are able to fly as fast as thirty miles per hour.

Hummingbird feeding on a flower ▶

Fact 45

Living in forests and meadows, hummingbirds fly from flower to flower, using their long, pointed beaks to sip nectar. Hummingbirds often collect nectar from as many as one thousand flowers in one day!

◀ *Ruby-throated hummingbird*

Big Birds

Fact 46

The ostrich is the largest bird in the world. Although it cannot fly, the ostrich can run about forty miles per hour—faster than any other bird!

◀ *African two-toed ostrich*

Fact 47

One ostrich egg is about the size of twenty-four chicken eggs! Ostrich chicks are already twelve inches tall when they are born. Adult ostriches can grow to be a few feet taller than most grown-up people!

Ostrich chick ▶

Fact 48

If an ostrich feels threatened, it kicks. Ostriches use their strong and powerful kick to protect themselves against animals like lions.

◀ *Ostrich*

29

Penguin

Fact 49

Most penguins are black-and-white birds that live in the cool waters south of the equator.

At twenty-two miles per hour, gentoo penguins are the world's fastest-swimming birds!

King penguins at the beach in the rain ▼

Fact 50

A group of penguins living together is called a rookery. Living side by side with many other penguins allows them to huddle together and stay warm.

◀ *King penguins*

Gentoo penguins ▶

Fact 51

Penguins are excellent swimmers, but they cannot fly. They use their flippers to paddle through the water and to keep their balance when waddling across slippery surfaces such as wet rocks or ice.

Fact 52

Usually, female penguins lay one egg at a time. Male and female penguins take turns caring for the egg. A female penguin often will go hunting for food while the male keeps the egg warm.

◀ *A penguin with an egg*

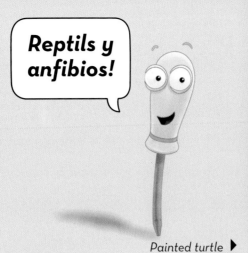

Painted turtle ▶

Reptiles & Amphibians

Both reptiles and amphibians are cold-blooded. Their bodies have the same temperature as their surroundings.

▲ A green tree python hatching

Born or Hatched?

Most reptiles and amphibians hatch from eggs. Amphibian eggs do not have a hard protective shell like reptile or bird eggs do.

◀ Green iguana

What Are Reptiles?

Reptiles are animals that are covered with scales. Scales are rough, dry pieces of skin that protect a reptile's body.

No, Pat, a reptile is a type of animal. Such as this snake!

Reptiles? Those are the square things we use to cover bathroom floors, right?

Not *tiles*, *reptiles!*

Red eyed tree frog ▶

What Are Amphibians?

Amphibians are animals that don't have hair, fur, feathers, or scales. They have wet, smooth skin. Most amphibians live in or around water because they must keep their skin a little wet.

33

Alligator

Fact 53 Alligators are reptiles that live in swamps, marshes, rivers, and lakes. Alligators have bumpy, scaly skin, four webbed feet, and long tails.

S-s-see you later, alligator!

American alligators ▼

34

Fact 54

When searching for food, the alligator swims with just its eyes and nostrils above the water.

◀ *Alligator head resting on the water*

Fact 55

Alligators use their webbed feet and long, powerful tails to paddle through the water. Although they have about eighty teeth, alligators do not chew their food. Once they capture prey in their powerful snouts, alligators swallow it whole.

Fact 56

Alligators lay forty to fifty eggs at a time in nests made of mud, leaves, and plants. When it's about to hatch, a baby alligator will make a high-pitched croaking sound to let its mother know it's ready to leave the egg and join the world!

◀ *American alligator hatchling*

Chameleon

Blue looks good on you, too!

Fact 57 Chameleons are lizards that can change the shade of their skin to almost any color in the rainbow. Scientists believe they change their color based on their mood or in reaction to changes in light and temperature.

Jackson's chameleon ▼

Fact 58

Chameleons can turn their eyes separately in any direction. They can look behind them without turning their heads and even look forward with one eye and backward with the other!

◀ *Chameleon hidden by leaves*

Fact 59

Chameleons are one of the few types of lizards that have a prehensile, or grasping, tail. They use this special tail to wrap around branches as they climb trees.

Fact 60

Chameleons have very long, sticky tongues that they can quickly flick in the air to catch insects. Their tongues are sometimes twice the length of their bodies.

◀ *This baby veiled chameleon is picking up a fly with his tongue.*

Ball Python

Fact 61

The ball python is a snake that can grow to be between three and five feet long. It is also known as the regal or royal python.

Ball python ▼

Fact 62

When baby ball pythons hatch from their eggs, they are called hatchlings. The average ball python hatchling is sixteen to eighteen inches long.

◀ *Ball python hatchlings*

Fact 63

Ball pythons have a shy and gentle nature. When they get nervous, ball pythons curl up into tight balls, hiding their heads inside.

Ball python, curled into a ball ▼

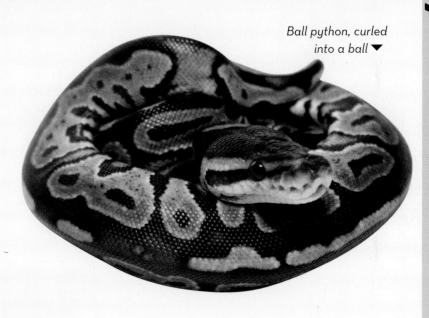

Fact 64

Ball pythons are very good at hunting for food on the darkest nights. They have heat-sensing pits in the scales near their mouths and eyes that can sense when animals are nearby. This helps them find and catch prey even when they can't see it clearly.

◀ *Ball python*

Big

Fact 65
The giant tortoise is one of the longest-living animals on earth. Many of them live for more than 150 to 200 years! The giant tortoise can grow to be six feet long and almost 500 pounds

◄ *Giant tortoise*

Fact 66
To rid themselves of ticks and other bugs, giant tortoises get some help from birds. The tortoise will raise itself up on its legs and stretch out its neck to invite birds to rest on its head and remove any pests that might be on its body.

Giant tortoise ▶

Fact 67

If a tortoise senses danger, it will hide its head, neck, and legs inside its hard shell. Unlike turtles, tortoises spend their lives on land. They eat shrubs, grasses, and even cacti.

◄ *Galapagos giant tortoise*

Small

Fact 68

The poison dart frog is an amphibian. They capture spiders, ants, and termites with their long, sticky tongues. Poison dart frogs range from less than an inch to two and a half inches in body length.

◄ *Blue-and-black poison dart frog*

Fact 69

Unlike other frogs, the male poison dart frog cares for his babies by watching over the eggs. Once they hatch, tadpoles swim onto the dad's back, and then he carries them to a safe spot where they can continue to grow.

Orange-and-black poison dart frog ▶

Fact 70

The poison dart frog—also called the poison arrow frog—got its name from native South American tribes, who used the poison on the frogs' skin to make their blowgun darts.

◄ *Peruvian poison dart frog*

Pez!

Orca ▼

Sea Creatures

Sea creatures are animals that live in or around the sea.

What Are Sea Mammals?

Some sea creatures are mammals. Sea mammals can't stay underwater all the time. They have to come to the surface to breathe air.

California sea lions ▼

What Are Fish?

Fish are creatures that live in the water and have gills to help them breathe. Most fish have fins to help them swim.

We're talking about sea creatures, Rusty, animals that live in the sea or *océano*.

I can't wait to learn about sea creatures!

You see creatures?! W-w-where do you see creatures? Yikes!

What Other Animals Live in the Sea?

Other sea creatures like crabs and lobsters have shells, long arms, or sharp claws and stay underwater most of the time.

Sally Lightfoot crab ▶

Puffer Fish

Fact 71

The puffer fish, also known as the blowfish, gets its name because its body puffs up to twice its normal size when it feels threatened. It puffs up quickly by swallowing water.

Puffer Fish are carnivores, which means they only eat meat.

Puffer fish ▼

44

Fact 72

The puffer fish keeps a very strong poison in its liver, muscles, and skin that protects it against its enemies.

◀ *A pufferfish that perceives danger*

Fact 73

Puffer fish have beaks similar to a bird's beak. They eat sponges, clams, sea urchins, and corals by grinding them down with these strong beaks.

Porcupine fish ▶

Fact 74

In its normal state, the puffer fish is tube-shaped. When blown up, the puffer fish is shaped like a big ball. Some puffers have smooth skin, while others have spikes.

◀ *Juvenile puffer fish*

Dolphin

Fact 75 Dolphins are sea mammals, which means they live in the water but must come to the surface to breathe.

Dolphins usually sleep with one eye open.

Bottlenose dolphin ▼

46

Fact 76

Dolphins live together in family groups of ten or twelve dolphins. These groups are called pods.

◀ *A pod of dolphins*

Fact 77

As soon as baby dolphins are born, they swim up to the surface to breathe air and then return to drink their mothers' milk. Baby dolphins stay with their mothers for three to six years before joining a pod of other young dolphins.

A mother dolphin jumping out of the water with her calf ▶

Fact 78

Dolphins are friendly, playful animals that are very close to other members of their pods. If a dolphin is having trouble breathing, the other dolphins in the pod will work together to help it reach the surface so that it can get air.

◀ *A baby Atlantic bottlenose dolphin with its mother*

So Many Teeth!

Fact 79
Sharks are fish that have been on the earth a very long time. In fact, they were around 100 million years before dinosaurs lived!

◀ *Great white shark*

Hammerhead shark ▶

Fact 80
Unlike other fish, sharks do not have bones. Like our noses and ears, sharks' skeletons are made of cartilage. Sharks, however, do have sharp, bony teeth. If a tooth is damaged or lost, a shark can grow a new one. A typical shark has about 30,000 teeth throughout its lifetime.

▼ *Zebra shark*

Fact 81

> Just like sharks, I can't wait to sink my teeth into things!

There are many different kinds of sharks. Some grow to be the size of a pencil, while others can grow to weigh as much as two elephants! Most sharks, though, are the size of people.

So Many Legs!

Fact 82
The name octopus means "eight feet." Each of its eight arms has two rows of suction cups, which help it pry open shells. If the octopus loses one of its arms, it can grow a new one!

▲ Young octopus

Fact 83

The octopus uses its arms to catch crabs, fish, turtles, shrimp, and other octopuses. It then uses its parrotlike beak to inject a venom into their prey.

Octopus gliding through the water ▶

Fact 84
Octopuses move along the bottom of the oceans by walking on their arms, gripping the ocean floor with their suction cups. To move quickly through the water, octopuses use jet propulsion: they expel water from their body to move themselves along.

◀ Red octopus

Sea Otter

Fact 85 Growing three to six feet long, sea otters are covered with brown or black fur that's thicker than any other mammal's fur.

See otters? No, I don't see any otters!

Alaskan sea otter ▼

Fact 86

Sea otters eat shellfish, clams, and sea urchins. They'll often use rocks to smash open the shells of their prey. Sea otters will only eat their food while floating on their backs.

◀ *A Sea otter carrying food*

Fact 87

Sea otters like to float together on their backs in groups called rafts. Rafts may include a group of all-male otters or a group of mothers and their pups.

Sea otters holding hands ▶

◀ *Sea otter*

Fact 88

The fur on their hands and necks will lighten in color as they get older, turning almost white. Otters are the only sea mammals that do not have blubber! The air trapped between the thick layers of their fur keeps sea otters warm.

Sea Horse

Fact 89

Sea horses can be red, orange, yellow, gray, blue, or green. They might be solid-colored or have patterns, such as spots or zebralike stripes. Sea horses can change colors to blend in with their surroundings.

Where does this horse's saddle go?

Sea horse ▼

Fact 90

Male sea horses carry their babies' eggs inside their pouches until they're ready to hatch. The daddy sea horse is the only male in the animal kingdom known to give birth. Baby sea horses are called sea ponies.

◀ *Rare sea horse*

Pregnant sea horse ▶

Fact 91

Like opossums, chameleons, and many monkeys, sea horses have prehensile tails. Prehensile tails act like hands; they are used for holding or gripping objects.

Fact 92

Sea horse couples stay together for life. To greet one another, they turn a brighter color. They often swim side by side with their tails hooked together.

◀ *A couple of sea horses*

Honeybee ▶

Spider ▲

Bugs & Cool Crawlers

Most bugs and cool crawlers have exoskeletons, which means their skeletons are on the outside of their bodies.

Stag beetle ▶

What Are Arachnids?

Arachnids are animals with eight legs, such as spiders, scorpions, and ticks.

S-s-spiders?!

What Are Insects?

Insects are animals with six legs. Many of them have wings and antennae.

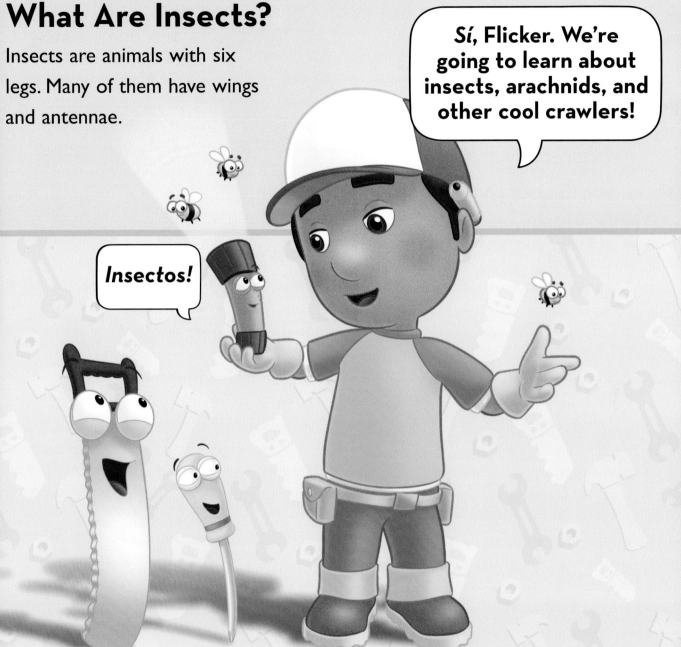

Insectos!

Sí, Flicker. We're going to learn about insects, arachnids, and other cool crawlers!

Red colored millipede ▶

Other Cool Crawlers

There are also plenty of animals that don't have six legs or eight legs. Millipedes and centipedes have between 30 and 200 legs, worms have no legs, and snails have one big leg called a foot.

Ant

Fact 93

Although they are small, ants are incredibly strong insects. Some ants can carry objects that are twenty times their size!

Fire ants are dark red ants that can sting and cause skin to feel as if it's been burned.

Leaf-cutter ant ▼

56

Fact 94 Ants live in underground nests in big groups called colonies. Their nests have long tunnels and several chambers, or "rooms." There's a room where the ants eat, a room for storing food, a nursery area, and rooms for sleeping.

◄ *Ants bringing food into their nest*

Fact 95 Ants use their antennae, or feelers, to communicate with each other. When two ants touch feelers, they are usually telling each other where to find food.

Fact 96

Ants have strong, scissorlike jaws that open and shut sideways. Since they can't eat solid foods, ants squeeze out all of the liquids from food and leave the leftover solid parts behind.

Tarantula

Fact 97 The world's biggest (and hairiest) spider is the tarantula. While some grow to be as small as a bottle cap, the largest ones can be as big as a dinner plate!

Seeing a tarantula up close can be a *hair-raising experience!*

Mexican red knee tarantula ▼

Fact 98

Tarantulas live in warm climates such as hot, dry deserts or humid rainforests. Most live in burrows in the ground, but some live in trees.

◀ *Tarantula*

Fact 99

If disturbed by other animals, tarantulas from North and South America have hairs on their backs that they can rub off using their back legs. These hairs will stick to the other animals, and make their enemies very itchy!

Red knee tarantula ▲

Fact 100

Tarantulas are venomous, but their venom won't seriously harm humans. If a tarantula were to bite a human, the effect would be no worse than a bee sting.

◀ *A woman holding a tarantula*

59

Scorpion

Fact 101 Just like spiders and ticks, scorpions are members of the arachnid family. They have tiny hooks at the end of each of their eight legs.

Escorpión!

Emperor scorpion ▼

Fact 102

Scorpions have two huge pincers near their heads and a curved tail with a venomous stinger on the end.

◀ *Emperor scorpion*

Fact 103

Many scorpions are found in warm, dry areas, such as the desert, where tracking down food and water can be difficult. Scorpions usually eat insects, lizards, and rodents, but if food is hard to find, they can survive on just a few meals a year!

Scorpion in a defensive position ▶

Fact 104

Baby scorpions are born bright white! Adult scorpions are black, brown, or reddish-black. A mother scorpion carries her babies on her back for several weeks.

◀ *Baby scorpions*

Caterpillar

Fact 105 A caterpillar is a baby butterfly or moth. Most caterpillars have sixteen legs and spend most of its time eating leaves and flowers. As it eats, a caterpillar gets bigger and bigger.

◀ Caterpillar

Fact 106 When we grow, our skin grows with us—but did you know that a caterpillar's skin doesn't grow with it? As a caterpillar grows, it needs to shed its skin. This is called molting. Caterpillars shed their skin four or five time before becoming adults.

Caterpillar ▶

Fact 107 A caterpillar has a mouth and strong jaws that help it eat leaves. It eats and grows until it becomes a pupa. Then it stays inside the pupa as it grows into a butterfly.

◀ Monarch chrysalis

Butterfly

Fact 108

Some butterflies have brightly colored wings, while others have dull-colored wings. These color patterns serve a special purpose: they help to warn predators that the butterflies taste bad!

Fact 109

Butterflies do not have mouths to bite into food. Instead, they drink flower nectar through a strawlike tube called a proboscis, which looks like a long, black tongue.

Blue Salamis butterfly ▶

Fact 110

Butterflies smell with their antennae and breathe through tiny holes along the sides of their bodies. They also use their feet to taste food. Butterflies have special sensors on their feet that let them "taste" the flower or fruit they're standing on!

◀ *Monarch butterfly*

Little Einsteins Fact Page

They may be considered among the scariest-looking animals on the planet, but these creatures are truly amazing members of the animal kingdom! Here are some frightfully fun facts about these featured creatures.

A female black widow spider has a red or orange "hourglass" on her belly.

Black Widow Spider

FACT 112 Most spiders make spiderwebs. They build them from silk. The black widow's silk is stronger than that of almost any other spider.

Bat

FACT 111 Even though bats have wings, they are not birds. Bats are mammals, just like humans. The bones in their wings are similar to those in our arms and hands, and they even have small thumblike claws on their wings to grasp things.

Kiwis can outrun most humans! They are related to emus and ostriches, which are also fast-running birds that can't fly.

Bats are very social animals, and mother bats will often babysit each other's pups.

If you see a white cockroach, that means it's just shed its skin!

Cockroach

FACT 113 Cockroaches are tough insects. They can live without food for a month and can live without their heads for about a week!

Jellyfish

FACT 114 Jellyfish don't have eyes, ears, a brain, or even a heart! Even so, they are able to capture food by using their long poisonous tentacles to sting fish.

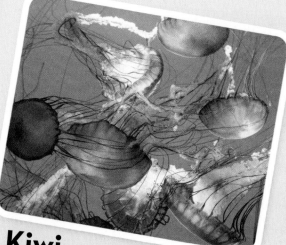

Kiwi

FACT 115 Kiwis are birds that live in New Zealand. They are each about the size of a chicken and have long beaks and no tails. Kiwis' wings are only two inches long, so it's no wonder they can't fly!

Anaconda

FACT 116 Anacondas can be found in swamps, lakes, and rivers of South America. They are the largest snakes in the world. Anacondas can grow to be twenty feet long and can weigh up to 300 pounds!

Snail

FACT 117 It looks as though snails crawl along on their bellies, but the bottom part of a snail is really its foot.

Sloth

FACT 118 Sloths are known for being the world's slowest animals! They live in the rainforest and can sleep twenty hours a day.

Turkey

FACT 119 Each turkey has a fleshy wattle under its beak and a fleshy flap of skin called a snood that hangs over its beak. Both turn bright red when the turkey is upset.

◀ *Leaves*

Seasons

A season is a period of time during the year. There are four seasons in one year: spring, summer, fall, and winter.

◀ *Crocuses*

Seasons Around the World

When it is summer in one part of the world, it could be winter in another!

How Long Is a Season?

Each season is about three months long. The seasons change slowly, going from spring to summer to fall to winter, and back to spring again.

Every season is my favorite season, thanks to sweet summer squash, crisp fall apples, winter white turnips, and lovely spring daffodils!

Seasons Change

In some parts of the world, the weather changes when the seasons change. The types of plants that bloom and the behavior of animals also can change from one season to the next.

Spring

Fact 120 In some parts of the world, the weather gets warmer when spring arrives, helping to melt away winter's snow and ice.

What do bees buzz about in spring? Why, lots of honey, of course!

Fact 121

In spring, the days grow longer, which means it stays light outside later into the evening.

Fact 122

In spring, many flowers start blooming. Trees that have rested all winter long begin growing leaves and opening buds. Spring often brings lots of rainy days, which are good for helping plants grow.

Wild blue crocuses blooming ▶

Fact 123

Birds, frogs, and many other animals are born in spring. It's also a busy time for honeybees, which buzz from flower to flower collecting the nectar they need to make honey.

◀ *Honeybee gathering nectar*

Summer

Summer is lots of fun in the Hundred-Acre Wood. What is summer like where you live?

Fact 124 In some parts of the world, summer arrives in late June, and it's hot and sunny outdoors. The days grow even longer than the days in spring. In some places, it stays light outside all through the night!

Fact 125

In the summer, many trees are covered with big green leaves, providing us with shade from the sun. Grass grows tall this time of year, and the sweet smells of roses, lilies, and other summer flowers often fill the air.

Fact 126

Bees and butterflies land on the flowers of fruit and vegetable plants to collect nectar. The insects spread pollen and help the flowers grow into tasty summer fruits and seeds to grow new plants.

Monarch butterflies ▶

Fact 127

During the hot summer months, insects such as ladybugs, mosquitoes, and fireflies can be seen flying here and there. Have you ever seen a firefly where you live?

◀ *Ladybug*

71

Fall

Fact 128

In fall (also called autumn), the weather gets cooler and the sun sets earlier in the day.

Bouncing in crunchity fall leaves is what Tiggers do best!

72

Fact 129

When the days get shorter and it begins to get chilly outside, some animals know that it's time to start gathering nuts and berries to eat during the cold winter months.

◀ *Squirrel*

Fact 130

In some places, leaves start to change colors in fall, becoming bright red, yellow, or orange. As the weather gets even colder, these leaves will fall from the trees and turn brown and crispy.

Fact 131

Many delicious fruits and vegetables—such as apples, yams, beets, pumpkins, lettuce, cabbage, grapes, chestnuts, turnips, broccoli, pears, and winter squash—are ready to be picked in fall.

◀ *Apple tree*

Winter

Oh, dear, I hope I have enough carrots to make my carrot soup, stew, and muffins this winter

Fact 132
By the time winter arrives in some parts of the world, autumn's colorful leaves have fallen and the trees are bare. During winter, frost often appears on the grass in the morning.

Snowman ▼

Fact 133

In many places, winter is the coldest time of the year. It can get very windy, snowy, and icy outside. Ponds and lakes may freeze and turn to ice.

Fact 134 Winter days are very short. The sun sets early in the evening, and, without the sun's light to warm the air, the temperature gets colder.

Fact 135 Some animals, such as this least weasel, change their appearance in winter. This weasel's brown coat turns white in winter. The white fur helps it blend in with snow and stay hidden from predators. In spring, the least weasel will shed its white coat for a brown one again.

◀ *Weasel*

75

Snow on trees ▲

Weather

When we talk about weather, we're talking about what the air is like in a certain area. Is the air hot and dry? Is it cold and damp?

Changes in the Weather

Weather is always changing. It changes from hour to hour and day to day. People who study the weather are called meteorologists. A barometer, such as this one, is one instrument used to predict the weather.

Barometer ▶

What Is Weather?

Weather is made up of different things, such as wind, temperature, sunshine, and clouds.

What Affects the Weather

Water that is in the air affects the weather. Without water, there could be no clouds, rain, lightning, or snow!

Lightning strikes ▶

77

Cloud

It's just another cloudy day for me.

Fact 136 There is water in the air that you can't see. This "invisible water" is called water vapor. When water vapor rises high into the sky, where it is very cold, the vapor forms a cloud!

Fact 137

Some clouds look like big puffs of cotton. These are called cumulus clouds. Cirrus clouds are thin and curly, while stratus clouds look like long, flat layers of white. Can you tell which types of clouds are pictured here?

◀ *Cumulus clouds*

Fact 138

Dark gray clouds are called nimbus clouds. When you see nimbus clouds filling the sky and making it dark, it means it's ready to rain. *Nimbus* means rainstorm, which is why these clouds are also called rain clouds.

Nimbus clouds ▶

Fact 139

A combination of the words cumulus and nimbus, a cumulonimbus cloud is a large, dark, and puffy cloud that's electrically charged. Cumulonimbus clouds are better known as thunderclouds!

◀ *Cumulonimbus clouds*

Rain

Rain forms when the vapor that forms clouds turns into droplets of water and falls from the sky.

See that gray nimbus cloud, Roo? That means it's about to rain.

Fact 141

Raindrops can come down in a gentle sprinkle or in heavy sheets that sometimes cause leaves and flowers to break off from stems.

Fact 142

Rain soaks into the ground, giving trees, grass, flowers, fruits, and vegetables the water they need to grow.

Spring flowers in the rain ▶

Fact 143

Some rain soaks deep into the earth. Humans use wells and underground pipes to bring that rainwater up out of the ground to use in our homes. This is some of the water that comes out of our faucets!

◀ *Old-fashioned water pump*

Hailstones

Fact 144 Hailstones are lumps or balls of ice that fall from the sky. They are formed when raindrops pass through an area of cold air on their way to the Earth.

Large hailstones ▼

82

Fact 145

Hailstones range in size, with most falling between the size of gum balls and golf balls. The largest hailstone ever recorded was the size of a large grapefruit. It was nearly seven inches long and weighed almost two pounds!

◀ *Hailstones*

Fact 146

Areas of India and Bangladesh have reported some of the largest hailstones in the world. In North America, the city of Cheyenne, Wyoming, has about nine or ten hailstorms every summer!

Large hailstones ▶

Fact 147

Because hail falls at speeds of fifty to seventy miles per hour, it can cause serious damage to houses, cars, and trees. It can also seriously injure people and animals!

Lightning

It's simply electrifrying!

Fact 148 There are millions of water droplets in rain clouds. During a storm, the activity of the droplets rubbing against each other creates electricity. This is called lightning!

Fact 149

Every second of every day, there are fifty to one hundred instances of lightning striking the ground somewhere in the world!

◀ *Summer lightning storm*

Fact 150

The temperature of a lightning bolt is hotter than the temperature of the sun! Since lightning heats the air so quickly, a bolt makes the cold air around it shake with a loud sound, called thunder. Have you ever heard thunder during a storm?

A thunderstorm moving across the open country ▶

Fact 151

If you listen closely to the sound of thunder, you can tell how close the lightning is. If it's far away, you may hear a low rumble or no sound at all. But the closer the lightning gets, the louder the crackle or bang it makes!

◀ *A powerful lightning bolt*

Rainbow

Fact 152

When the rays of the sun and misty sheets of rain come together in the sky, a rainbow sometimes appears. Have you ever seen a rainbow?

I wonder if there's a golden honeypot at the end of that rainbow.

Rainbow ▼

Fact 153

Colors in a rainbow always appear in the same order: red, orange, yellow, green, blue, indigo and violet.

◀ *Rainbow on the coast*

Fact 154

You don't need a rainy day to see a rainbow. If you watch water spraying from a garden hose on a summer day with the bright sun behind you, you may see a rainbow in the mist!

The wind is blowing droplets of water to form a rainbow over this fountain. ▶

Fact 155

At times, you can see a double rainbow in the sky—a bright rainbow and a second, lighter-colored rainbow above it. The colors in the lighter rainbow always appear in the opposite order of the bright rainbow!

◀ *Full double rainbow*

Snow

When it comes to snowflakes and Pooh bears, no two are alike!

Fact 156

In cold temperatures, clouds will form ice crystals instead of raindrops. These crystals become heavy and fall to the ground as snow.

Fact 157

All snowflakes have six sides, but no two snowflakes look exactly alike. When it's very cold out, snowflakes are small, long, and thin. When it's warmer, they're larger and have more detailed designs.

Fact 158

Snowflakes begin as ice crystals that are as small as specks of dust. As they fall, the crystals connect to other crystals and form snowflakes. Some snowflakes look like flowers, stars, spiderwebs, or even lightning bolts.

Fact 159

In the Arctic, there are some people who live in houses made of snow. These houses are called igloos. Even though they're made using big blocks of snow, igloos keep people warm inside by keeping hot air trapped inside and the cold out.

◀ Igloo made from blocks of snow

Ice

Don't mind me. It's just the way I skate.

Fact 160

Ice is water that has frozen. In very cold temperatures, the water in ponds, lakes, and puddles turns to ice. Ice is smooth and slippery to the touch, and is usually clear or bluish-white.

Patterns of frosty ice ▼

Fact 161

Did you know that fish don't usually freeze when a lake or pond freezes over? Ponds and lakes freeze from the top down. The fish can continue to swim at the bottom of the lake or pond, far beneath the top ice layer, all through the winter.

Fact 162

In winter, you might see icicles hanging from trees or rooftops. Icicles form when dripping water freezes quickly. When the weather gets warmer, icicles melt.

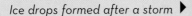

Ice drops formed after a storm ▶

Fact 163

The North Pole and the South Pole are the two coldest places in the world. They are both so cold that most of the water there stays frozen and icy all through the year!

◀ *Adelie penguin*

Wind

Fact 164 Although you can't see the wind, you can feel it moving through the air. Wind can be very strong and powerful, making leaves and kites zip through the air, or it can feel like a soft, gentle whisper against your skin.

Windy days are perfect for flying kites.

Fact 165 Sometimes we use the wind's energy to make machines and vehicles move. Windmills are farm machines that use the wind's energy to collect water or chop up grain, while sailboats use the wind's force to glide across the water.

◀ *Windmills*

Fact 166 The wind carries plants' seeds from one place to another. Wherever the seeds fall, they have a chance to grow into new plants. Many of the flowers and plants you see around you may have grown from seeds that were blown there from miles away.

Dandelion ▶

Fact 167 The windiest place on Earth is Port Martin, Antarctica. For a month, it has winds blowing as fast as sixty-five miles an hour. That's as fast as a speeding car!

Tornado

Fact 168

When warm air from the ground rises and hits cool air in thunderclouds, it can cause a swirling, funnel-shaped cloud. When this cloud touches the ground, it becomes a tornado.

Tornado at the end of the road ▼

A tornado touching down

Fact 169

Although a tornado may only last a few minutes, it can quickly and easily destroy trees, houses, and anything else in its path.

Fact 170

Tornadoes spin and move very quickly. The wind inside tornadoes usually moves in speeds between 50 and 115 miles per hour. Most tornadoes are about 250 feet wide and will travel a few miles before they die down.

Tornado ▶

Fact 171

When a very strong wind is mixed with heavy rains, it can form a hurricane. Like tornadoes, these stormy winds can knock down buildings and trees. A hurricane's wind can blow as fast as 250 miles per hour. That's as fast as an airplane!

◀ Damage from a tornado

Bodies of Water

Water is everywhere. People drink it, fish live in it, and birds bathe in it.

What Is Saltwater?

The water found in the ocean is saltwater. Lobsters, whales, dolphins, clams, and sea stars are just a few of the animals found living in the ocean's saltwater.

Sea star ▲

Lobster ▶

Water, Water Everywhere.

Water drips, flows, and splashes. It can be forceful, such as a fast moving river, or calm and silent, such as a lake.

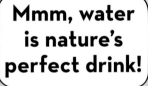

Mmm, water is nature's perfect drink!

Every living thing needs water to grow.

What Is Freshwater?

The water in lakes, ponds, rivers, streams, marshes, and swamps is called freshwater. Many different fish, reptiles, and amphibians live in freshwater.

Trout ▶

97

Lakes and Ponds

Fact 172

A lake is a large body of water that looks like a big swimming pool. Some lakes are very deep. Ponds are smaller than lakes and aren't as deep.

This is my favorite way to keep cool on a really hot day!

Canada ▼

Fact 173 Lakes and ponds are home to many interesting plants and animals. You can find frogs, beavers, ducks, turtles, snakes, cattails, reeds, and flowering lily pads living in or around lakes and ponds.

◀ Ducklings

Elk cooling in a lake ▶

Fact 174

Unlike the ocean, the water in lakes isn't constantly moving and crashing as waves; it's actually very smooth. The wind, however, can create tiny waves that are called ripples.

Lake Baikal, Russia ▼

Fact 175

Lake Baikal in Siberia is the world's deepest lake, measuring one mile deep. It is also the world's oldest lake—it's 25 million years old! Lake Baikal is also home to the world's only freshwater seals.

Rivers and Streams

Hoo-hoo-hoo! It's fun to splishedy-splashedy down the river.

Fact 176 Rivers are large, long bodies of flowing freshwater, and streams are small bodies of flowing freshwater.

Fact 177

Rivers and streams don't flow in a straight line. They twist and turn as they flow. Rivers start in the mountains or hills and usually end up flowing into a large body of water, such as an ocean, bay, or sea.

◀ *Curvy river*

Fact 178

Rivers can be deep and fast-moving or shallow and slow. Some rivers are muddy and brownish, while others are crystal clear.

River valley ▶

Fact 179

The Nile River is the longest river in the world. It is 4,184 miles long! Located in Africa, the Nile flows through nine countries and empties into the Mediterranean Sea.

◀ *Boats on Nile River*

Waterfalls

Fact 180

When water from a river rushes over a high cliff and pours down, it's called a waterfall. The force of a waterfall is very strong.

Angel Falls, Venizuela ▼

Fact 181

Niagara Falls is probably the best known waterfall in North America. Every second, 3,160 tons of water flow over the falls at a speed of twenty miles per hour!

◀ Niagra Falls

Fact 182

Many power stations use waterfalls to create electricity. As the water from these waterfalls flows through underground pipes, the force of it spins the wheels and gears of engines to help create electrical power!

A small dam and power plant in Norway ▶

Fact 183

The highest waterfall in the world is called Angel Falls. It's located in the country of Venezuela on a *tepuy* or flat-top mountain. Angel Falls is more than 3,000 feet high!

◀ Havasu Falls, USA

Marshes and Swamps

Fact 184 Marshes and swamps are bodies of water often found near rivers and lakes.

It's the insects, frogs, birds, and fish that make the swamp so noisy. Another mystery is history!

Wet marsh ▶

Fact 185

Marshes and swamps are shallow and muddy, and they are filled with all kinds of plants and animals. Marsh water is typically six inches to three feet deep, while water in swamps may be an inch to a foot deep.

◀ *Freshwater tidal wetlands*

Fact 186

Although very few trees grow around them, marshes are surrounded by grasses, reeds, and cattails. Crayfish, frogs, turtles, egrets, dragonflies, and snails are commonly found living in and around marshes.

Blue heron ▶

Fact 187

Swamps are warm, wet areas surrounded by many trees. Alligators, crocodiles, anacondas, shrimp, toads, woodpeckers, and mosquitoes are just a few of the animals that live in swamp areas.

◀ *Alligator*

Ocean

Fact 188

Oceans are very large bodies of water. When you go to the beach, you can see the ocean waves roll in and out, crashing against the seashore. Have you ever tasted ocean water at the beach? It is very salty.

Today's a perfect day for the beach!

Fact 189

There are five oceans in the world: the Arctic, Atlantic, Indian, Pacific, and Southern. The Pacific Ocean is the biggest ocean in the world. In fact, it almost goes all the way around the world!

◀ *The Great Barrier Reef in Australia*

Fact 190

Ocean waves are caused by gusts of wind. The size and strength of waves depend on how fast the wind is blowing, where it's blowing, and how long it's been blowing.

Wave ▶

Fact 191

Swells are stable and constant waves that have been created by storms. Swells may travel thousands of miles before they finally reach land! Swells are the waves that surfers love to ride.

Glaciers and Icebergs

Just what is an iceberg? I'm sleutherin' for some cold, hard facts!

Fact 192 Glaciers are like huge rivers of ice. Big chunks of this ice can break off and fall into the ocean, where they are called icebergs.

Dawes Glacier, Alaska, USA ▼

Fact 193

Glaciers can be hundreds of miles long, while icebergs are often as big as mountains. Icebergs are even bigger than they look, because more than half of an iceberg is hidden under the water!

◀ Icebergs

Icebergs from the Vatnajokull glacier, Iceland. ▶

Fact 194

Icebergs are often found in the North and South Pole regions, where it is very cold. Newfoundland and Greenland are two countries where you'll see many icebergs.

Fact 195

When icebergs melt, they make a fizzing sound. This sound is caused by the release of air bubbles, some of which have been trapped inside the ice for thousands of years!

Geysers

Wow, that geyser can jump higher than I can!

Fact 196 Geysers are created when hot water spurts out of holes in the earth. Like the water in a teakettle, the water deep inside the earth gets warm. When it gets very hot, the water shoots up into the air.

Castle geyser ▼

Fact 197 Old Faithful, located in Yellowstone National Park in the United States, is the most famous geyser in the world. Some geysers shoot water out (or erupt) every hundred years or so, but Old Faithful erupts nearly every hour!

◀ Old Faithful geyser

Fact 198

There are only about 1,000 geysers in the world, and more than half of them can be found in Yellowstone National Park

Cold-water geyser ▶

Fact 199 All geysers are found near active volcanic areas—a volcano's heat warms up the water.

◀ Great Fountain geyser

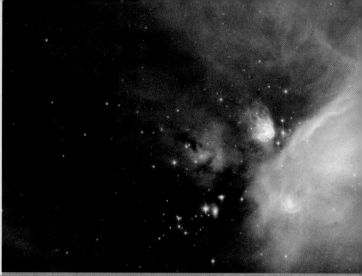

Up in Space

We call the area outside the Earth's atmosphere "space."

◀ Saturn

What Are Planets?

Very far away, high up in the sky are big, round objects called planets. There are eight planets in the solar system, including our planet, Earth.

Jupiter ▶

Where Are Planets?

The planets, sun, moon, and stars are very far away from us. We call the place where they're found "outer space."

Wouldn't it be fun to live on a planet?

But we do live on a planet, Roo. The planet we live on is called Earth

How Do We Learn About Planets?

Scientists who study outer space are called astronomers. They use telescopes to help them see faraway objects such as planets and stars.

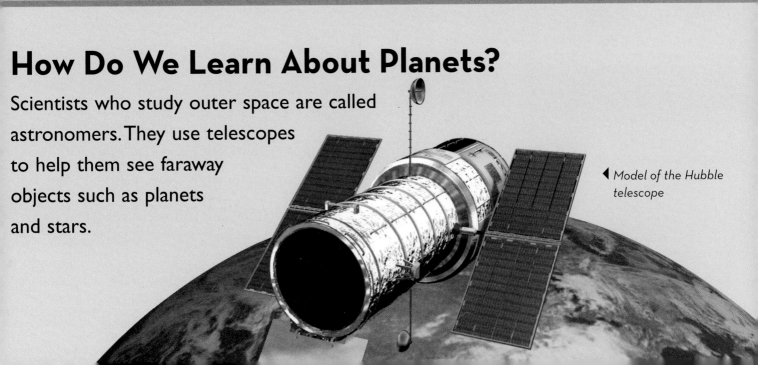

◀ Model of the Hubble telescope

Solar System

"Solar" means belonging to the sun. The sun is the center of the Earth's solar system.

Our solar system ▼

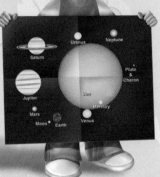

114

Fact 201 Our solar system includes the sun and the planets that travel around it. What else can you find floating around our solar system? About 400,000 asteroids: pieces of rock left over from the formation of the solar system nearly 4.5 billion years ago!

Fact 202 Earth, the planet we live on, is one of eight planets that travel around the sun. The other seven planets are Mercury, Venus, Mars, Jupiter, Saturn, Uranus, and Neptune. Some planets have moons, too, such as Jupiter, shown here with four of its moons.

Jupiter and its moons ▶

Fact 203

Each planet takes a different amount of time to circle around the sun. The period of time it takes for the Earth to travel around the sun is called one year, and each year lasts 365 days.

Earth

Fact 204

We all live on the planet called Earth. Earth is the only planet we know of with people and animals living on it.

I wonder how much of the world is covered in honey!

Solar flare ▼

Fact 205

Although you can't feel it, the Earth is constantly spinning. At the equator, the earth spins around 1,000 miles per hour. It takes twenty-four hours (a whole day) for the Earth to spin around one time.

Fact 206

As the Earth is spinning (rotating), it's also making its long, 365-day trip around the sun. Believe it or not, the Earth moves at a speed of thirty miles per second!

The international space station ▶

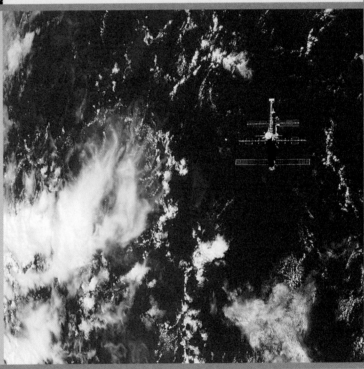

Fact 207

The Earth is made up of more water than land. Oceans cover almost three-quarters of the Earth's surface! Earth is often called the Blue Planet because of all the water that covers it.

Star

Fact 208

Stars are glowing balls of gas that twinkle in the night sky. Since they are so far away, they can look like little white dots, but many stars are a million times bigger than our sun!

Stars ▼

Hoo-hoo-hoo! How about a constellation called the Big Tigger?

Fact 209

Constellations are stars that appear to form familiar shapes in the sky, like connect-the-dot puzzles. Many constellations are shaped like animals or people.

Fact 210

One of the brightest constellations is the Big Dipper, which looks like a pan with a very long handle.

The Big Dipper ▶

Fact 211

Large groups of stars are called galaxies. A galaxy might be made up of billions of stars! The Earth, sun, and the rest of our solar system are just a tiny part of the Milky Way Galaxy.

◀ *Galaxies*

Sun

My garden needs water and plenty of sunshine to help it grow.

Fact 212 Did you know that the Sun is a star, just like the ones we see lighting up the night sky? The Sun is much closer to Earth than any other stars, so it looks much bigger and brighter. The Sun is so close to the Earth that we can feel its warmth.

Golden sunset ▼

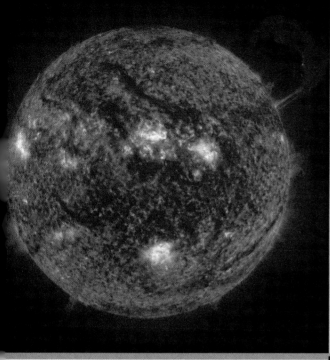

Fact 213

Without the Sun, there wouldn't be any life on Earth; our planet would be dark and frozen, and wouldn't have any plants or animals. Like all living things, we need the Sun's light, heat, and energy to survive and grow.

◄ *Solar flare*

Fact 214

Although it looks small in the sky, the Sun is actually much bigger than Earth. In fact, the Sun is about a million times bigger than the Earth. If the Earth were the size of a pinhead, the Sun would be the same size as a soccer ball!

Earth with the rising Sun ▶

Fact 215

As Earth rotates around the sun, different areas of the planet feel the Sun's heat more than others. Some places are experiencing winter, while others are going through the summer season. What season is it now in your part of the world?

◄ *Sunset*

Moon

Fact 216

When you see the Moon at night, it seems to be shining, but the Moon doesn't give off any light of its own. It is actually a dull gray color, but it looks bright white to us because it reflects light from the sun.

Nighttime sky in a forest ▼

Mama told me that the moon changes shapes in the sky! What does the moon look like out your window tonight?

Fact 217 As the Moon travels around the Earth, the sun shines on it at different angles, changing the way the Moon looks in the sky. Depending on the night, the Moon might look like a circle, a half circle, or even a crescent.

◀ *Crescent moon*

Surface of the moon ▶

Fact 218

The surface of the Moon has many deep holes, called craters. When viewed from Earth, the biggest craters make a dark pattern that almost looks like a face on the Moon. Can you see the "face" on the Moon?

Fact 219 Six of the eight planets in our solar system have one or more moons! Earth has one, Mars has two, Neptune has eighteen, Uranus has twenty-seven, and Saturn has sixty. This is Io, one of Jupiter's sixty-three moons.

◀ *Io, a moon of Jupiter*

Meteor

Fact 220 Meteors are actually rocks from space that appear as streaks of light in the night sky. As the rocks enter Earth's atmosphere, they start to burn up and glow. This is why meteors are often known as "shooting stars."

Perseid meteor ▼

Let's make a wish on a shooting star.

124

Fact 221

Did you know that most meteors are not that large? Big meteors can be the size of a basketball, while small meteors are about the size of a grape.

◀ *Metorite fragment*

Fact 222

Small meteors are often dust particles from a comet, while larger meteors are usually broken bits of asteroids or planets. Meteors that survive the trip through Earth's atmosphere and land on the ground are called meteorites.

Barringer Crater, Arizona, USA ▶

Fact 223

Meteors may heat up to 3,000 degrees Fahrenheit when they enter Earth's atmosphere! When large meteors explode and cause a bright flash in the sky, they are called fireballs. The explosion from a fireball can be heard up to thirty miles away!

◀ *Meteor shower*

Comet

Fact 224

Comets are large objects in space made up of ice and dust. Comets are often called "dirty snowballs."

Comet Hale Bopp over Stonehenge, UK ▼

Hey, that comet has a Tigger-ific tail—just like I do!

Fact 225

Millions of comets can be found zipping around at the edge of our solar system, beyond the outermost planets.

◄ Comet Hale Bopp over Grand Teton National Park, USA

Halley's Comet ▶

Fact 226

If two comets bump into each other, one of them may fly into our solar system, and that's when we can see it in the sky.

Fact 227

Comets have what look like long, glowing tails following them. As a comet gets closer to the sun, its ice and dust start to vaporize and get loose, leaving a bright trail in the night sky.

◄ Comet Ikeya Zhang

Little Einsteins Fact Page

Climb aboard and get ready to explore! The Little Einsteins are taking a trip on their favorite rocket ship through the solar system. They've gathered some fascinating facts about the eight planets that are simply out of this world!

Neptune's Great Dark Spot—a huge, spinning storm about the size of Earth—was first seen by the Voyager 2 spacecraft in 1989, but it was gone in 1994 when the Hubble Space Telescope looked for it again.

Astronomers have been watching Jupiter's Great Red Spot for at least 400 years!

Mercury and Venus are the only two planets in the solar system that don't have moons orbiting them. The planet with the most moons is Jupiter, which has sixty-three moons.

Mercury

FACT 228 Even though it's about 28 million miles away, Mercury is the closest planet to the sun! Mercury travels around the sun faster than any other planet in our solar system.

FACT 229 Mercury looks a lot like our moon. It's very rocky and has lots of craters, but is a little bit bigger than our moon.

Venus

FACT 230 Venus is the only planet in the solar system that spins toward the right, which is called clockwise.

FACT 231 Venus has more volcanoes than any other planet in the solar system. Scientists are not sure if the volcanoes are no longer active or if they'll erupt in the future.

Mars

FACT 232 Mars is called the red planet because of its rocky, orange-red soil. Known for its many dust storms, Mars' sky always looks pink or pale orange in color.

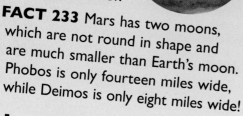

FACT 233 Mars has two moons, which are not round in shape and are much smaller than Earth's moon. Phobos is only fourteen miles wide, while Deimos is only eight miles wide!

Jupiter

FACT 234 Jupiter is the largest planet in the solar system. It's so big that 1,300 Earths could fit inside it!

FACT 235 Jupiter is known for its Great Red Spot, which is actually a huge, hurricane-like storm with winds reaching 270 miles per hour.

Saturn

FACT 236 Saturn is a large planet known for its hundreds of colorful rings. The rings are actually made up of ice, dust, and bits of rock.

FACT 237 The planet Saturn takes about thirty Earth years to revolve around the sun. It travels at a speed of almost 22,000 miles per hour!

Uranus

FACT 238 Uranus is the third-largest planet in the solar system. About sixty-three Earths could fit inside Uranus.

FACT 239 Uranus is surrounded by twenty-seven gray moons.

Neptune

FACT 240 Of all the planets, Neptune has the craziest weather. It has really big storms with very fast winds, some of which have reached 1,500 miles per hour!

FACT 241 Due to its deep blue color, the planet Neptune was named after the Roman god of the sea. Neptune has thirteen moons.

Pluto

FACT 242 Beginning in 1930, Pluto was considered to be the ninth planet in our solar system. But due to its small size and irregular orbit, astronomers decided to classify it as a "dwarf planet" in 2006.

FACT 243 It takes Pluto about 248 Earth years to orbit around the sun once.

Eggplant ▶

Plants

Trees, grass, and flowers are all plants. Fruits, vegetables, and leaves all come from plants.

Corn growing in summer ▲

What Do Plants Look Like?

Plants come in many different colors, shapes, and sizes. A plant can be as tiny as your fingertip or as tall as a house!

Sunflower ▶

What Are Plants?

Most plants have roots, stems, and seeds. Nearly all plants have leaves.

> Gawrsh, Daisy, I couldn't find that 'egg plant' you were looking for, so I made one for you!

> That was awfully nice, but I think *this* is the eggplant Daisy was looking for.

> An eggplant is a fruit, because it forms from a flower and has seeds.

What Makes Plants Grow?

All plants need light, water, and air to grow. Plants are the main source of oxygen production on Earth, since they release more oxygen back into the air than they use.

Potted and hanging plants ▶

131

Seed

Most plants—from tall trees to tiny flowers—start off as seeds. Seeds grow in the soil. Seeds first sprout roots, which grow downward and anchor the seeds in the soil.

Have you ever blown dandelion seeds into the air?

Ear of paddy ▼

132

◀ *Seedling poking through the soil*

Fact 245

After getting plenty of water and warmth, a little stem starts to poke out of the top of the seed, pushing its way up and out of the soil. Soon the stem may grow leaves and become a big plant!

Watermelon ▶

Fact 246

When you cut into many fruits, such as cucumbers, tomatoes, watermelons, and apples, you can see their tiny seeds!

Fact 247

Have you ever seen squirrels gathering acorns? Acorns are actually the seeds of oak trees! All oak trees begin as little acorns.

◀ *Acorns*

133

Leaf

Hey, *leaf* me alone!

Fact 248

A leaf is part of a plant. Most plants have leaves, which grow out from plants' branches and stems. The leaf's job is to make food for the plant.

Big green leaf ▼

Fact 249 Leaves can look like hearts, ovals, fans, triangles, needles, and many other shapes. They can have pointed or rounded edges, and can be smooth, fuzzy, or even prickly to the touch.

◀ *Leaves on a vine*

Fact 250

Mixed salad leaves and herbs in a bowl ▶

If you have ever eaten lettuce or spinach, then you've tasted plant leaves! You've probably also tasted herb leaves, such as mint, rosemary, basil, and oregano, which add flavor to many of the foods we eat.

Fact 251

The biggest leaves can be found on the raffia palm tree. They can grow to be sixty-five feet long. That's nearly as long as a tennis court!

◀ *Raffia palm*

135

Flower

Fact 252

Flowers are the pretty blossoms on plants. They come in many colors, shapes, and sizes. They grow in the woods, in gardens, in parks, and in yards.

Wet tulips ▼

Fact 253

The sunflower is one of the tallest flowers in the world. Some have grown to be more than twenty-five feet tall! Tiny seeds grow in the middle of sunflowers. Have you ever eaten sunflower seeds?

◀ *Sunflowers*

Fact 254

Many flowers, such as roses, lilacs, and lilies, smell very sweet. Bees, hummingbirds, and butterflies are attracted to the color and smell of flowers and drink their sweet nectar.

Monarch butterfly ▶

Fact 255

The stinkiest flower in the world is the rafflesia flower. It attracts a lot of flies, because it smells like rotting meat.

◀ *Rafflesia flower*

Grass

Fact 256 Grass grows in places such as parks, yards, and fields. There are more than 10,000 types of grass! Grass isn't always green; it comes in a variety of colors, sizes, and textures.

This grass skirt is perfect for dancing the hula.

Dune grass ▼

Fact 257

A lot of the foods you eat, such as oats, rice, and wheat, are grasses. Even sugar comes from the stem of a grass called sugarcane.

◀ *Golden wheat*

Fact 258

Many animals, such as cows, horses, and sheep, eat grass. Grass can also be woven into baskets and is used in some countries to make roofs for houses.

Fact 259

Bamboo is the tallest grass in the world. It grows very fast. In fact, it can grow as much as one foot in a single day!

◀ *Bamboo*

Tree

There are two types of trees: deciduous and evergreen. The leaves of deciduous trees start growing in spring, turn colors in fall, and drop off in winter. Evergreen trees, such as pine trees, keep their leaves all year.

Know how to get a chipmunk's attention? Run up a tree and act like a nut!

Changning leaves on trees ▼

Fact 261

Trees are homes for many animals. Some build their nests on tree branches; others live in holes in trees or sleep in hollow logs that have fallen on the ground.

◀ *Bald eagle in its nest*

Fact 262

The wood from trees can be used to build houses, boats, fences, and furniture. Most of the paper we use—from newspapers and coloring books to cardboard boxes and toilet paper—comes from trees!

Home construction ▶

Fact 263

You can look at a slice of a tree trunk and count the rings to determine how old the tree is: one ring equals one year!

◀ *Rings of a tree trunk*

Garden

Fact 264

A garden is an area, usually outdoors, where people plant and grow plants.

Garden ▼

Fact 265

You don't need a large backyard to grow a garden. In fact, many people plant gardens in pots or window boxes.

◀ *Flower box*

Fact 266

A garden can have fruits, vegetables, flowers, or all of these kinds of plants growing together. Gardens need sun, water, and lots of care and attention.

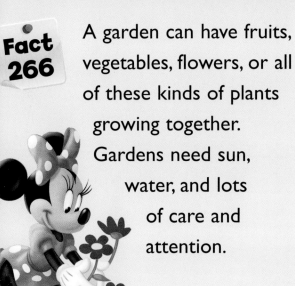

A boy watering flowers ▶

◀ *Weeding a garden*

Fact 267

Weeds are plants that grow in gardens and steal water and nutrients from the soil. That makes garden plants weak. Gardeners should pull out weeds regularly to keep their garden plants healthy and strong.

Vegetable

Fact 268 Vegetables are the parts of plants that we can eat! Lettuce is one plant's leaves; celery is another's stem; broccoli is a flower; and beets are roots. Vegetables are healthy foods that are full of vitamins and nutrients.

Vegetable cart in front of a greengrocer ▼

Fact 269

Not all vegetables are green. Many come in bright colors, such as red radishes, orange pumpkins, yellow squashes, and purple eggplants.

◀ *Radishes*

Fact 270

Carrots are crunchy orange vegetables that are good for your eyes. If you eat plenty of carrots, they can help you to see better!

Carrots ▶

Fact 271

The tomato is really a fruit! Scientifically speaking, it has all the characteristics of a fruit. But because the tomato is often used as a vegetable and is not sweet like most fruits, many people consider the tomato a vegetable.

◀ *Tomatoes*

Fruit

Now where did that banana skin go? Keep your eyes peeled, boys!

Fact 272
A fruit is a part of a plant we can eat that contains seeds. Some fruits have several seeds, while others have one large seed that can be found inside their pit.

Freshly ripened peaches ▼

Fact 273

Fruits can be soft and sweet like bananas, tart and crispy like apples, or even sour and juicy like lemons.

◄ *Mixed berries*

Glass of lemonade ▶

Fact 274

Fruits contain lots of vitamins and minerals. Many drinks are made with fruit, such as lemonade, fruit punch, grape juice, orange juice, and apple juice.

▼ *Granny Smith apple*

Fact 275

There are more than 7,000 different kinds of apples. One is even named after a grandma. Maria Anne Smith, an Australian grandmother, was the first person to grow the type of apple called a Granny Smith!

Cactus

Fact 276 Most plants need a lot of water to grow, but the cactus is able to live in the hot, dry desert where little rain falls. The cactus stores any rain that does fall in its thick, fleshy, wax-coated stem.

Cacti in the desert ▼

Fact 277

Cactus plants, or cacti, are covered with sharp spines. These spines keep desert animals from eating the plants, shade the plant, and collect dew.

◀ *Barrel cactus*

Fact 278

Some cacti look like small pincushions, while others are shaped like barrels or stubby fingers. Many cacti have colorful flowers.

Cactus in bloom ▶

Fact 279

The Saguaro cactus has curving branches that look like arms. Saguaros can grow as tall as a five-story building and can live for more than 200 years!

◀ *Saguaro*

149

Mushroom

Fact 280

Although they grow in forests, gardens, and backyards, mushrooms are not plants; they are fungi. Unlike plants, fungi don't need sunlight to grow.

Mushrooms ▼

150

Fact 281

Mushrooms grow in many colors—including white, yellow, red, and brown—some have large, round caps that grow on thick stems. They feel soft and spongy to the touch.

◀ *Amanita muscaria*

Fact 282

Mushrooms grow in warm, damp, shady areas. You can usually find them growing on logs and leaves, in the wet soil beneath trees, and even on trees themselves.

Mushrooms on a log ▶

◀ *Dark truffle mushroom*

Fact 283

Truffles are very special, rare mushrooms that grow beneath the forest floor. These difficult-to-find fungi are prized by chefs. Some truffle lovers train dogs and pigs to track down tasty truffles by smell!

Medium pueblo mud houses ▶

Mobius Arch, Alabama, USA ▲

Land

Land, the solid part of Earth's surface, is all around us. Whether as big as a mountain or as small as a backyard, all land is made of the same things: rock, sand, and soil!

Who Lives on the Land?

Certain animals live in the land. For example, bats live in caves, and gophers live inside underground burrows.

Prairie dog ▶

Uses for Land

Most people use elements of land—such as stone, clay, and soil—to build their homes.

What Grows from the Land?

A lot of the food we eat grows from the land. Farmers grow fruit trees in their orchards and vegetables in their fields.

Orange grove ▶

153

Rock

This is what I call *rock and roll!*

Fact 284 Rocks are made up of minerals, which are tiny grains of crystals or metals. When minerals are squeezed or pressed together, they form rocks!

Multicolor stones ▼

Fact 285

Rocks can be small, such as the tiny pebbles you find in a stream, or as big as a mountain. Some rocks are grainy and dull, and others are shiny and sparkly.

◀ *Balancing stones*

Fact 286

People use rocks to build walls, walkways, houses, and many other kinds of buildings. Rock is a good material to build with, because it is so heavy and strong.

The Alamo in San Antonio, Texas, USA ▶

Fact 287

While many rocks are rough and jagged, you'll find the smoothest rocks in oceans, brooks, and rivers where water is constantly running over them and rounding their rough edges.

◀ *Nightcap Ranges National Park rainforest*

Sand

Fact 288 Sand is actually tiny bits of rocks and seashells that have been worn down by wind and water. Sand feels rough and gritty between your fingers.

The beach is a perfect place for a *sandwich*, isn't it, Uncle Donald?

Sand castle by the sea ▼

Fact 289

Many deserts are filled with sand. When the wind blows, it pushes the sand into piles, creating hills called sand dunes. Some of the highest sand dunes in the world are found in Africa.

◀ Sand dunes

Fact 290

If you look around your neighborhood, you'll probably find many things made from sand, such as bricks, cement, roof shingles, paved streets, sidewalks, and driveways.

Back bay facade ▶

◀ Glass artist at work

Fact 291

When it is heated up to an extremely high temperature, sand turns into a liquid. When this hot liquid sand cools, it becomes glass! Windows and mirrors are made from sand.

Soil

Just as I suspected: when soil gets wet, it turns to mud!

Fact 292 Soil, is another important part of land. It's made from a mixture of bits of rocks and decayed plants. Soil is found on Earth's surface.

Sprouts growing from the soil ▼

Fact 293

Plants need soil to help them stand up tall and strong, and to keep their roots safe. Soil also has nutrients and water that help plants grow.

◄ *A plowed field prepared for new planting*

Fact 294

Clay is a special kind of soil. It's smooth and moist, and easy to shape into pottery. Once the pottery is baked in a hot oven, it hardens and can be used as vases, plates, and cups.

Potter decorating a spinning pot ▶

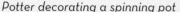

Fact 295

Loam is a gritty, sticky soil that forms in puddles. Certain birds, called swallows, search for puddles and collect loam from them. Then the swallows use the loam as "glue" for building their nests.

◄ *Four young swallows in a nest*

159

Shell

Fact 296 Shells are the exterior skeletons of a group of soft-bodied animals called mollusks.

Ouch! I guess this shell isn't empty after all!

A variety of seashells ▶

◀ *Clamshell*

Fact 297

Shells are very important to the mollusks inside them, giving them protection and sometimes camouflage from their enemies.

Fact 298

Shell shapes have different purposes. Cone-shaped shells are good for tunneling underground; smooth, spiral shells glide through wet, heavy sand; and ridged shells help anchor mollusks to the ocean floor.

Seashell ▶

Fact 299

A shell grows as the animal living inside it grows. Once the animal leaves, the shell stops growing.

◀ *Hermit crab*

Cave

Fact 300 Caves are natural openings in rocky sides of hills or cliffs. All caves are damp and dark. Many are deep enough to have waterfalls and lakes inside them.

Sea Caves, Cape Greco, Cyprus ▼

Fact 301

Long ago, people used to live in caves. They drew pictures about their lives on the cave walls.

◄ Bushmen paintings and rock art

Fact 302

A mixture of water and rock minerals constantly drips from cave ceilings. When the water dries up, the minerals harden into rock formations that look like icicles!

Cave with stalagtites ►

Fact 303

Some animals live inside caves. During the day, hundreds of bats may sleep close together in the same cave, hanging from the cave ceiling by their feet!

◄ Group of bats in the underground cave

Mountain

Fact 304 Mountains, which are made of rock and soil, stand tall above the rest of the land. It takes millions of years for mountains to form. There are still mountains forming all over the world.

Mountain climbing has its ups and downs.

Reflection of Teton Range on Beaver Pond at sunrise ▼

Fact 305

Mountains are home to many animals. Wild goats climb the rocks; mountain lions hunt for animals; and eagles soar over the mountaintops, building their large nests along cliffs.

◀ *Mountian goat with kid*

Fact 306

Many people enjoy exploring mountains. In winter, it's fun to ski down snowy mountain slopes. In summer, people enjoy camping and hiking on mountain trails.

Skiing ▶

Fact 307

The top of a mountain, or peak, is its coldest spot. Many times you'll see snow on mountain peaks, even in summer! The highest mountain peaks do not have any plants or trees.

◀ *Himalayas, Nepal*

Volcano

A volcano is a mountain that forms around a hole, or vent, in the ground. This hole is so deep that it connects to the hot liquid rock that's far below Earth's surface!

What a *lava-ly* volcano!

Volcanic eruption ▼

Fact 309

When enough pressure builds up, the hot liquid rock bursts up and explodes through the top of the volcano. This liquid rock is called lava.

◀ *Volcanic eruption*

Fact 310

Lava is a very hot liquid that can reach temperatures of more than 2000 degrees Fahrenheit! The word "volcano" comes from the name of the Roman god of fire, Vulcan.

Lava flowing ▶

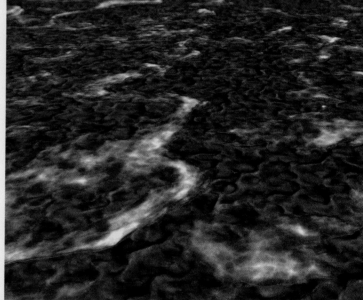

Fact 311

The largest volcano on Earth is Hawaii's Mauna Loa. It is about six miles tall from the sea floor to the opening. However, the largest volcano in our solar system is Olympus Mons on the planet Mars. It is about seventeen miles tall!

◀ *Mauna Loa volcano, Hawaii USA*

167

Canyon

Fact 312

Created by rivers, canyons are very deep valleys with steep, rocky sides. Over thousands of years, a river's steady flow of water forcefully carves into the land, eventually forming a canyon.

That's a great canyon.

It's the *Grand* Canyon.

Fact 313

The largest canyon in the world is in the United States: the Grand Canyon. It's so big— one mile deep and 277 miles long—that it can be seen from outer space!

◄ North Rim of the Grand Canyon, Arizona

Fact 314

The sides of the Grand Canyon are made up of many colorful layers of rock. The rock layer at the very bottom of the canyon was formed almost two billion years ago!

Colorado River through the Grand Canyon, Arizona ►

Fact 315

Valles Marineris, located on Mars, is a canyon that is truly out of this world! Even bigger than the Grand Canyon, Valles Marineris is an amazing 2,500 miles long and five miles deep!

◄ Valles Mariners, Mars

Gold

Fact 316 Gold is a soft, shiny, bright yellow metal that can be used as money or to make jewelry, sculpture, and even fillings for teeth!

Gee, people say I'm as good as gold, but I don't think I look that expensive.

Gold bars ▼

Fact 317

When people think of gold, they often think of riches and wealth. But did you know that gold is actually a mineral that's found underground?

◀ *Gold running through rock*

Fact 318

After gold is mined, or dug out of the ground, it is usually melted down. Once melted, it can be shaped into beautiful jewelry, watches, or other items.

Pieces of gold ▶

Fact 319

Gold is a rare metal, which means it's hard to find. Yellow gold is very special, because it's the only metal that won't rust or change color over time!

◀ *Gold chains and necklaces*

171

Gems

Fact 320 The beautiful gems used in jewelry are actually minerals and rocks! Some of the most popular gems include red rubies, blue sapphires, green emeralds, and clear diamonds.

Gems, including sapphires, emeralds, rubies, tanzanite, and tourmaline ▼

Fact 321

To polish gems, gemologists (scientists who work with gems) "tumble" the rocks. After four or five weeks in a machine that mixes the rocks together with sandy grit, the rocks come out shiny and polished.

◀ *Rocks and minerals*

Fact 322

Many of the gems that people wear as jewelry today were formed a billion years ago! Some gems can be found 100 to 300 miles beneath Earth's surface.

Quartz ▶

Fact 323

Diamond is the hardest substance in the world. If you want to cut a diamond in half, you have to use another diamond to do it!

◀ *Diamonds*

Habitat

Habitats are specific environments where plants and animals with similar needs live.

Crab underwater ▲

What Is in a Habitat?

Habitats can be cold and icy, hot and dry, or damp and rainy. Some habitats are under the water and others are underground.

Gorilla in the grasslands ▶

What Are Habitats?

A habitat contains everything a group of plants and animals needs to survive: just the right amount of light, air, water, soil, food, and shelter.

> **Polar bears are suited to living in this habitat. They have furry coats and a layer of fat, called blubber, under their skin.**

> **Gawrsh, I'd be blubbering all the time if I lived in this habitat!**

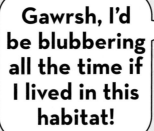

What Lives in a Habitat?

Plants and animals are suited to live in their habitats. For example, camels and cactus plants need little water to survive, so they're suited to living in the hot, dry desert.

Camels in the desert ▼

Taiga

Fact 324 A taiga is a forest that's mostly made up of conifer trees. Conifers are evergreen trees that grow cones, such as pine, juniper, cedar, spruce, and redwood trees.

Taigas are forests that are filled with evergreen trees.

Taiga forest in Canada ▼

Adult reindeer browsing lichen

Fact 325

Taigas are found in the cold, northern parts of Europe, Asia, and North America. The animals that live in taigas, such as reindeer, arctic foxes, and caribou, must be able to survive harsh winters.

A little gray squirrel sitting at the bottom of a tree ▶

Fact 326

Squirrels and other animals sometimes carry cones to other parts of the taiga. When the seeds from the cones take root, the forest grows.

Fact 327

The Siberian taiga is the largest forest in the world. It spreads across northern Russia and is as wide as the Atlantic Ocean!

◀ Karatosh, Siberia, Russia

177

Temperate Deciduous Forest

Fact 328

A temperate deciduous forest is a cool, rainy habitat mainly made up of trees that grow leaves in spring and then lose them in fall.

The canopy of an old oak tree ▼

Fact 329

There are five layers to a temperate deciduous forest. The tallest layer is called the tree stratum or canopy, which includes trees that can reach heights of eighty to 100 feet. The second layer is the small-tree layer, made up of shorter and younger trees.

◀ *Colorful foliage*

Fact 330

The third layer is the shrub layer (containing shrubs such as azaleas), while the fourth is the herb layer, which is made up of plants such as wildflowers and berries. Finally, the ground layer contains ground-hugging plants, such as moss.

Wild blueberries ▶

Fact 331

Mosses and lichens, which grow on the forest floor, are plants that have no roots and thrive in moist, shady areas. Moss also grows on many deciduous trees.

◀ *Snail*

Tropical Rain Forest

Fact 332 Tropical rain forests are warm, wet forests that are home to millions of different plants and animals. They are very important to humans, since rain forests create most of the Earth's oxygen that we breathe.

Aw, phooey! I don't think I'm blending into this habitat!

Canopy of the Amazon rainforest ▼

Fact 333

Tropical rain forests are found in Africa, Asia, Australia, India, and South America. Some rainforests get more than 100 inches of rain a year.

◀ *Gaudy leaf tree frog*

Natural moss growing on rocks ▶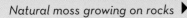

Fact 334

Trees in a tropical rain forest are so leafy and grow so close together that rain falling on treetops can take about ten minutes to finally reach the forest floor.

Fact 335

Australian rain forests are filled with unique flowers. About eighty percent of the flowers found in Australian rain forests cannot be found anywhere else on Earth.

◀ *Grevillea in bloom*

Prairie

Aaah! So many beautiful wildflowers grow on the prairie.

Fact 336

Prairies are areas of land filled with grasses, herbs, and wildflowers, but few or no trees. These dry, windy habitats can be found in the middle of the United States.

Pale purple cone flowers on a prairie ▼

Fact 337

Animals that live on the prairie, such as bison, prairie dogs, prairie chickens, and jack rabbits, often survive below-freezing winters and sweltering-hot summers.

◀ *Bison graising on the prairie*

Fact 338

Today, farms cover a lot of prairie lands. These farms produce many nutritious foods that feed both people and animals.

Hay bales ▶

Fact 339

The tall grasses of a prairie can grow between six and eight feet high. Some prairie plants have roots that reach ten feet beneath the surface of the soil!

◀ *Prairie flowers*

183

African Savanna

Fact 340 Grasslands in Africa are called savannas. Savannas are covered with tall grasses, but there are only a few trees scattered around.

African zebras ▼

184

Fact 341

Although they have a rainy season lasting several months, savannas are hot and dry the rest of the year.

◀ *African elephant*

Fact 342

Some savanna grass grows as tall as a grown-up human! Grass is an important food for animals such as zebras and antelopes, which spend their days grazing.

Antelope ▶

Fact 343

The African savanna is home to the world's fastest land animal (the cheetah), the world's largest land animal (the African elephant), and the world's tallest animal (the giraffe)!

◀ *Cheetah*

Australian Grasslands

Fact 344 The Australian grasslands are full of wildlife and plants, and dotted with farms, called "stations."

Sheep grazing on a farm in Southern New South Wales, Australia ▼

Fact 345

The animals living in the Australian grasslands have adapted to dry, windy conditions. Emus, kangaroos, wallabies, and wombats all do well in this environment.

◀ *Wallaby in a grassy paddock*

Fact 346

Kangaroo paw is a beautiful plant found in Australia's grasslands. Its flowers look like little kangaroo paws! Birds called honeyeaters drink the nectar from this plant's flowers.

Yellow kangaroo paw (Australian wildflower) ▶

◀ *Golden dingo pups*

Fact 347

Dingoes are wild dogs that live in the grasslands of Australia. They live in family groups called packs, which may have between three and twelve dogs. At night, packs hunt for rats, rabbits, lizards, birds, and kangaroos.

Tundra

Fact 348

The tundra is one of the coldest places in the world. Only the North and South Poles are colder. Tundra lands are found in the northernmost parts of Asia, Europe, and North America.

The sky over the tundra glows with colorful streaks of light called the northern lights!

Mountain tundra in Springtime, Colorado USA ▼

Fact 349

Tundra winters are freezing cold. The icy wind howls all day and night, and the land is frozen solid. The arctic fox, arctic wolf, polar bear, snowy owl, and wolverine all live in the tundra.

◀ Arctic fox

Fact 350

In some parts of the tundra, the summer is warm enough for plants to grow. The leaves of a tundra plant are usually tough, leathery, and dark red, green, or purple.

Red and green succulent in the alpine tundra ▶

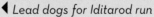

◀ Lead dogs for Iditarod run

Fact 351

The Iditarod is a sled race in Alaska that starts in Anchorage and ends in the tundra city of Nome. Siberian huskies and Alaskan malamutes work as a team to pull a sled over icy, snowy lands for more than 1,000 miles.

189

Desert

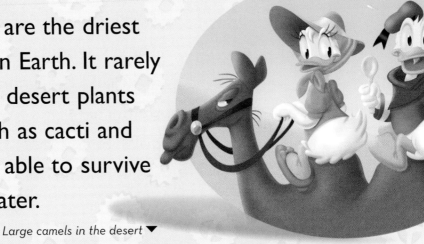

The desert? I thought we were going for dessert!

Fact 352 Deserts are the driest places on Earth. It rarely rains, so desert plants and animals—such as cacti and camels—must be able to survive with very little water.

Large camels in the desert ▼

Fact 353

When it does rain in the desert, a storm may last a few hours, and then it might not rain again for many months—or even years! A few weeks after a rain, bright wildflowers can appear in the desert.

◀ *Small desert flower*

A fennec, or desert fox, asleep against a rock ▶

Fact 354

Although a few deserts are cold during the day, most are very hot and dry. During daylight, many animals escape the heat by tunneling underground. At night, however, even the hottest deserts can drop to freezing temperatures.

Fact 355

Africa's Saharan desert is the largest desert in the world. It covers more than one million square miles!

◀ *Saharan desert landscape*

Little Einsteins Fact Page

The Little Einsteins have travelled around the world, meeting exciting animals and learning all about their unique habitats. Here are some of the cool facts they've collected about animal homes.

Barn

FACT 356 Some farm animals, such as horses and pigs, sleep in large buildings called barns. Instead of bedrooms, the barn has special areas called stalls where the animals sleep. Most farm animals sleep on beds of straw.

FACT 357 On the farm, chickens often live in buildings called coops. Chicken coops have perches and rows of nesting boxes where the chickens can lay their eggs.

Birds aren't the only animals that build nests. Reptiles and insects build them, too. And chimpanzees, gorillas, and orangutans build a new nest every night to sleep in!

Nest

FACT 358 Many birds live in homes called nests. Nests, which are shaped like cups or bowls, are cozy places for birds to lay their eggs and raise their babies.

FACT 359 A mama bird flies away from the nest to find worms and insects to feed her babies. Baby birds live in their nests until they are old enough to fly on their own.

Believe it or not, there's a bird that lives in a burrow! Burrowing owls live in tunnels that can be eight feet long and three feet under the ground.

Burrow

FACT 360 Many animals, such as gophers, groundhogs, moles, rabbits, salamanders, skunks, snakes, toads, and some squirrels, live in holes or tunnels in the ground. These holes are called burrows.

FACT 361 To make their tunnels, earthworms eat the soil as they burrow into it! Earthworms live in moist soil, often under rocks and logs.

Web

FACT 362 Spiders spin beautiful webs using a special silk that shoots from their bellies. If you've ever touched a spiderweb, you know that parts of it can stick to your fingers.

FACT 363 Spiders catch insects in their webs to eat. Spiders never get stuck in their webs thanks to the special claws they on their feet!

Did you know that spiders have silk-spinning glands called spinnerets that they use to create their webs?

Beehive

FACT 364 Honeybees live in homes called hives, which are made up of little, six-sided tubes or "rooms" called combs. Thousands of honeybees can live together in one hive.

FACT 365 Once bees collect nectar from flowers, they store the nectar in the combs where it changes into honey. This supply of honey is what the bees will live on in winter.

I cannot believe it! Did you know that people use beeswax to make candles, creams, furniture polish, lotions, and medicines?

Copyright © 2009 The Baby Einstein Company, LLC. All Rights Reserved. Little Einsteins logo is a trademark of The Baby Einstein Company, LLC. All Rights Reserved. EINSTEIN and ALBERT EINSETIN are trademarks of the Hebrew University of Jerusalem. www.albert-einstein.org. All Rights Reserved.

My Friends Tigger and Pooh are based on the "Winnie the Pooh" works by A.A. Milne and E.H. Shepard.

Written By Marcy Kelman. Vetted by Barbara Berliner, Fred Gerber—Director of Education Emeritus at the Queens Botanical Gardens, the experts at Disney's Animal Kingdom Theme Park at Walt Disney World Resort, and Dr. Andrew Fraknoi. Designed by Sequel Creative.

Photos by: Photos.com, iStockphoto, Image Source, Photodisc, Comstock, Getty Images, Agephotostock, Corbis, AP/Wideworld, and NASA.gov

Pleiades © Robert Gendler
Io © NASA
Panda Cub © Zoo Atlanta

Printed at RRDonnelley & Sons Willard, Ohio December 2009
ISBN 978-1-4231-1921-0